WE ARE ONE
UNDER THE SUN

WRITTEN BY JOCELYN MARIE SCHLEGEL

ILLUSTRATED BY JESSE MUSTO

This is a work of fiction. All of the characters, names, incidents, organizations, and dialogue in this novel are either the products of the author's imagination or are used fictitiously.

Illustrations by Jesse Musto.

WestBow Press books may be ordered through booksellers or by contacting:

WestBow Press
A Division of Thomas Nelson & Zondervan
1663 Liberty Drive
Bloomington, IN 47403
www.westbowpress.com
1 (866) 928-1240

Because of the dynamic nature of the Internet, any web addresses or links contained in this book may have changed since publication and may no longer be valid. The views expressed in this work are solely those of the author and do not necessarily reflect the views of the publisher, and the publisher hereby disclaims any responsibility for them.

Any people depicted in stock imagery provided by Thinkstock are models, and such images are being used for illustrative purposes only.
Certain stock imagery © Thinkstock.

ISBN: 978-1-9736-1439-5 (sc)
ISBN: 978-1-9736-1440-1 (e)

Library of Congress Control Number: 2017918936

Print information available on the last page.

WestBow Press rev. date: 12/13/2017

WESTBOW
P R E S S®
A DIVISION OF THOMAS NELSON
& ZONDERVAN

WE ARE ONE UNDER THE SUN

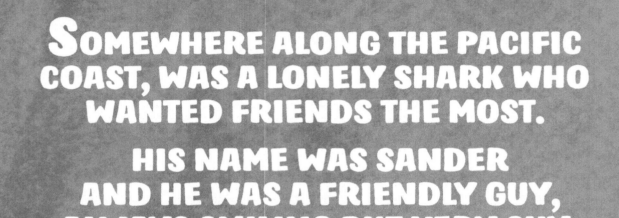

SOMEWHERE ALONG THE PACIFIC COAST, WAS A LONELY SHARK WHO WANTED FRIENDS THE MOST.

HIS NAME WAS SANDER AND HE WAS A FRIENDLY GUY, ALWAYS SMILING BUT VERY SHY.

He had trouble finding friends because of his big white teeth.

THIS MADE HIM SAD SO
HE HID UNDER THE REEF.

EVERY DAY HE SAW THE CHILDREN PLAY, AS THEY LAUGHED AND SPLASHED BUT THEY NEVER STAYED.

EACH WEEK A NEW FAMILY
VISITED THE BEACH.
THIS CAUSED SANDER TO
THINK FINDING FRIENDS
WAS A GOAL OUT OF REACH.

SANDER WENT TO HIS PARENTS
AND ASKED FOR ADVICE.

"ALL YOU CAN DO IS BE NICE!
LOOK FOR FRIENDS IN
OUR HABITAT," THEY SAID.
"YOU'LL THINK OF SOMETHING,
JUST USE YOUR HEAD!"

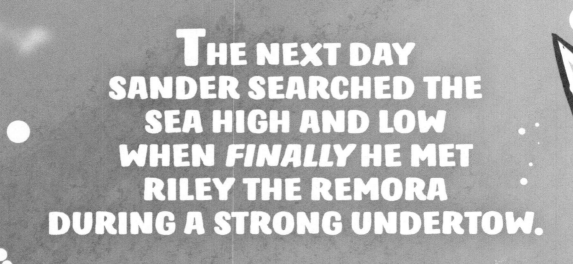

THE NEXT DAY
SANDER SEARCHED THE
SEA HIGH AND LOW
WHEN *FINALLY* HE MET
RILEY THE REMORA
DURING A STRONG UNDERTOW.

SANDER AND RILEY
SOON BECAME FRIENDS,
SWIMMING AND SINGING
UNTIL THE SUNS TIME TO SET.

SANDER ASKED RILEY WHY
THE CHILDREN DIDN'T WANT TO PLAY.
SHE TOLD HIM, "OUR HABITATS
ARE DIFFERENT, BUT THAT IS OKAY!"

"EVERYONE HAS A PLACE TO PLAY, OURS HAPPENS TO BE DEEP IN THE OCEAN UNDER THE SUN'S STRONG RAYS!"

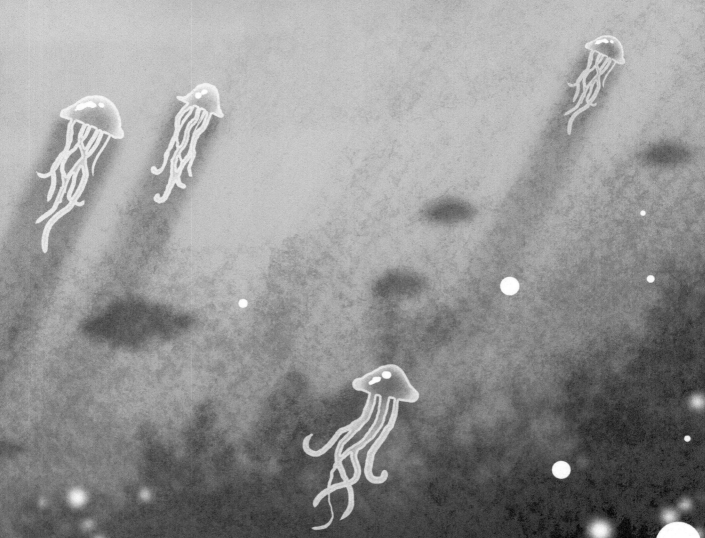

"**WE ALL HAVE OUR PURPOSE SO WE CAN MAKE THE EARTH BETTER, ALL HELPING EACH OTHER AND WORKING TOGETHER.**"

SANDER BEGAN TO MAKE
FRIENDS IN HIS HABITAT.
HE MET CREATURES OF
ALL SHAPES AND SIZES,
ROUND AND FLAT.

HIS NEW FRIENDS WEREN'T SCARED OF HIS TEETH. THEY ALL HAD SOMETHING DIFFERENT ABOUT THEM AS WELL, IT MADE THEM UNIQUE.

SOME OF HIS FRIENDS
GLOWED IN THE DARK.
SOME BLEW UP LIKE A BALLOON
WHEN THEY WERE TRYING TO
SCARE A BIG SHARK.

THEIR DIFFERENT TALENTS
WERE WHAT THEY ALL SHARED.
THEY LEARNED TO ENJOY
BEING RARE.

THEY SHOWED EACH OTHER THEIR DIFFERENT SKILLS, LIKE BLENDING IN WITH THE CORAL AND COUNTING THEIR GILLS.

SANDER QUICKLY LEARNED
THAT BEING DIFFERENT IS FUN.
BECAUSE AT THE END OF THE DAY,
WE ALL PLAY UNDER THE SAME SUN.

THE
END